# Scream Team

## The Zombie at the Finish Line

**by Bill Doyle**
**Illustrated by Jared Lee**

Scholastic Inc.

To L.L., N.H., and J.R., thank you for putting me in the game.
—B.D.

To Jerry Stevenson.
—J.L.

ISBN 978-0-545-47978-3

Text copyright © 2013 by Bill Doyle
Illustrations copyright © 2013 by Jared D. Lee Studio, Inc.

12 11 10 9 8 7 6 5 4 3 2 1     13 14 15 16 17 18/0

Printed in the U.S.A.          40
First printing, February 2013

Book design by Jennifer Rinaldi Windau

# CHAPTER 1
## "DUDE, YOU *STILL* LOOK LIKE A POODLE"

The rusty ball spun through the foggy night air. Bits of green mold and speckles of slime flew off it. And all Karl the werewolf could think was, *Chomp that ball!*

His paws thundered along the track as he raced after the shot put. Karl moved so fast that his patchy fur pressed flat against his face.

"No, Karl!" his best friend, J.D. the ghost, shouted from the long jump. Around the swamp's small track and field, other monsters stopped sprinting,

jumping, and throwing. They all gaped at Karl.

But he didn't care. Karl loved to run and he was so close now! Before the shot put could hit the ground, Karl leapt into the air. He opened his mouth wide and—

*Clang!*

His jaws clamped down on the metal ball. It was heavy and weighed down his snout.

"Umph!" he said, almost chipping a fang, but holding the ball tightly in his mouth. With his tail wagging, Karl trotted over to the shot-put circle. He spit the ball out in the mold and slime, at the paws of the big werewolf who had thrown it.

"Dude, you *still* look like a poodle," the werewolf sneered, and his voice brought Karl out of his daze.

*Wolfsbane*, Karl thought.

It was Alphonse. About twice Karl's size, Alphonse was the star of the Werewolves track squad. And he was one of the reasons Karl had started the Scream Team with eight other monsters.

Alphonse had made sure Karl wasn't welcome

on the Werewolves team during baseball season. And the other Junior Club Monster League teams had not wanted any of his friends, either.

"We meet again, poodle," Alphonse sneered.

"Meet again?" Karl said, wiping shot-put slime off his chin. "Wrong, Alphonse! This is the first *meet* of the track-and-field season!"

Rolling his eyes, Alphonse threw the shot put again. "Fetch!" he yelled. The metal ball squeaked as it left his paws.

Karl actually took a couple of steps, before forcing himself to stop. Alphonse always said that Karl's patchy coat made him look like a poodle. He didn't need to act like one, too.

But it wasn't easy. Karl chased squeaky things and his tail. Especially when he got nervous, like now. His team was about to go head-to-head with the Werewolves.

J.D., Bolt the Frankenstein's monster, and a few other Scream Team monsters rushed over to see if Karl needed help.

"Not cool, Alphonse!" Dennis the vampire said. But the drool, dripping down his oversize fangs, made it sound like, "Nosh shool, Salfonshe!"

"Speak it, don't leak it, bat boy," Alphonse said. He gave the Scream Team athletes a long look and laughed. "Wow, you're all even bigger losers than I remembered. We're going to crush you tonight, and then we'll win the Deadcathlon intra-*ghoul*-ral meet next week!" As he strutted over to his own team, he called back, "Be sure to ask your coaches about the Conundrum Cup C-U-R-S-E!"

For some reason, Alphonse spelled this last word. But Karl didn't really notice. His ears had perked up at *the Deadcathlon*. One of the biggest meets of the season, it took place over two nights with nine different events.

"We'll see you there!" Karl yelled after Alphonse. "The Deadcathlon is for the best teams and we're one of them! We'll get invited!" But a quick look around at his teammates, who were warming up for tonight's meet, didn't fill Karl with confidence. Eric the blob was stuck bouncing between two hurdles like a Ping-Pong ball. Maxwell the mummy dangled from the high-jump bar like a giant yo-yo.

And on the far side of the track, Patsy the zombie was acting nutty as she practiced her sprints. She was lightning fast, but whenever she got close to the finish line, she backed off like it was electrified.

"You have to cross the finish line!" Karl shouted. "Come on, Patsy, you can do it!"

"I know . . . I can do anything!" the zombie called back, but for once she didn't sound sure of herself. She still wouldn't cross the line.

"Where are the coaches?" J.D. the ghost asked. "Patsy will listen to them."

"Coaches fight," Bolt grunted. "There."

He pointed to the parking lot where Karl could see Virgil and Wyatt Conundrum. With two heads on the same monster, they shared a pair of arms and legs, but that was all they shared. They couldn't agree on anything, and Karl could hear them arguing . . . yet again.

"It's *track and field*, not *field and track*," Wyatt snapped at Virgil. "So clearly, track is better."

"*Field* sounds like *feelings*," Virgil chirped, his ponytail bouncing up and down. "And those are so super important."

"In track and field, *track* is the older part," Wyatt fired back. "And that's *more* important. Just like me."

Virgil chuckled. "Bro, we share the same birthday."

"Says who? Who's been talking about me?" Wyatt looked around suspiciously. "Them?" he demanded, pointing up at the stands. The spectators were mostly werewolves. But there was also a group of five monsters dressed in purple robes with hoods. Wyatt always thought spies were watching him.

"Your energy is bringing me down," Virgil said. "I'm going to meditate!"

"And I'm going to the van!" Wyatt said.

They pulled in different directions, spinning their body round and round.

"Where are they going?" Karl wondered out loud. The Scream Team watched the Conundrums twirl across the parking lot and down the street. Soon the bickering pair disappeared over a hill and was gone.

Ugh. The Conundrums were always having

fights, but this was a bad one even for them. He had to find a way to make them get along. He thought about something Alphonse had said.

"What's the Conundrum Cup C-U-R-S-E?" he asked Beck the bigfoot, spelling the last word.

J.D. overheard him and shouted, "Don't say that name!"

"What name?" Karl said. "Conundrum Cup Curse?"

Just as Karl said it, Patsy tried crossing the finish line and exploded.

# CHAPTER 2
## POP GOES THE ZOMBIE

*KABLAM!*

Patsy's body burst apart just before the finish line, like a favor at a birthday party. As if rocket-propelled, every piece shot off into the distance.

"This is not going as planned!" her head yelled as it sailed over a fence and into a nearby slug farm. Her knee flew into a tongue-tickler nest in a pus-bag tree. Her heel landed in the stadium's snot fountain.

Karl had seen Patsy fall to pieces hundreds of times. Getting tackled in football, walking while chewing gum, laughing at a monstrously bad joke.

But this was different. Like the Conundrums, Patsy was already having trouble with track season—especially around finish lines.

"Don't worry, Patsy!" Karl shouted. "We'll get you back together!" He and the rest of the Scream Team split up around the stadium to find her pieces.

"No, I'll do it!" Mr. Benedict, the team sponsor, told them. Without the coaches there, the shy mole man was in charge. "The first event starts in five minutes, and you have to get ready." As Mr. Benedict rushed off, he called over his shoulder, "I put your new track uniforms in the crate by the wrong jump!"

The Scream Team took turns going inside the crate to put on the track shorts and shirts. While they waited in line, Karl turned to J.D. and said, "Why did you tell me not to say *Conundrum Cup Cur—*"

Before he could say *curse*, J.D.'s body turned bright red. "Don't say it!" he yelled. "Or the C-U-R-S-E will strike!" he warned, spelling the word instead of saying it.

"What is the . . ." Karl paused, then said, "What is the thing that rhymes with *hearse*?"

"I'm not sure," J.D. said. "But it's bad enough that even saying it can cause catastrophe! I heard that the Coaches Conundrum were involved in a tragic track-and-field mystery at the first Deadcathlon. Something went horribly wrong and they haven't been back since."

Beck the bigfoot came out of the crate wearing the new shorts and T-shirt. Karl was surprised that the blue, shiny uniforms actually looked really good.

Karl was the last one waiting to change. As J.D. came out, he went in. "Is the thing that rhymes with *worse* the reason the Conundrums never won the Conundrum Cup?" The Cup was the trophy given to the top team at the Deadcathlon.

"No one knows!" J.D. said.

"Hmmm," Karl said. "I've got it! We just need to win the Cup for the Conundrums at the Deadcathlon next week. That'd finally make them happy and stop fighting!"

"The Scream Team wins the Deadcathlon?" J.D. laughed. "Good one, Karl."

Karl didn't laugh. He didn't want to think like Alphonse. He knew the Scream Team athletes weren't losers. They just needed a chance.

Karl couldn't wait to put his plan into action. He forgot all about spelling or rhyming as he burst out of the crate. "Winning the Conundrum Cup could break the Conundrum Cup Curse!" he cried.

*Phlurrp!* Just then, the moon came out from behind a cloud. And the team's shorts and shirts instantly shrank about three sizes.

"What's happening?" Karl gasped, as the uniforms kept shrinking. He felt like a bag of slime with a tightening string around the middle. And Eric looked exactly like that.

"I told you not to say *C-U-R-S-E*," J.D. said. His voice sounded strangely high, like a mite mouse's. "It has struck again!"

The team tried stripping off the uniforms, but they were too snug. Mike the swamp thing's shorts squeezed even tighter, turning his tail into a balloon. Dennis's tiny bat wings popped out and he zipped in circles like a three-winged gnat. Bolt the Frankenstein's monster groaned and toppled over. "Monster wedgie," he groaned.

Maxwell the mummy's T-shirt had shrunk, pushing more of his sweaty wrapping up around his head. It blocked even more of his vision than usual. "Be honest," he moaned. "Is this a good look for me?"

Mr. Benedict finally came back, his arms filled with Patsy's body parts. By then the Scream Team was rolling in the muck while the clothing squished them even more.

Patsy's head was tucked under Mr. Benedict's chin. Her eyes went wide when she saw her teammates. "What's going on?" she asked.

"Shrinking uniforms!" Karl grunted.

"Oh my!" Mr. Benedict mumbled, throwing his hands in the air in surprise. All of Patsy's parts fell to his feet.

"The uniforms are woven with live boa worms that shrink in moonlight," Mr. Benedict explained. "I thought they'd make great skintight uniforms. You know, aerodynamic."

Dennis flew face-first into the ground. "Not really," he said, his voice muffled by muck.

"The worms are going berserk," J.D. said. "How can we get the uniforms off?"

Mr. Benedict thought for a second. "Boa worms love to eat fried fungi. I'll just whip up a batch in the kitchen crate I brought. That will distract them and they'll let go."

"Great!" Karl said.

"Shouldn't take me more than ten minutes," Mr.

Benedict said, and then added, "Maybe an hour."

"The meet is about to start!" Karl shouted. He looked at the starting line, where the Werewolves were already gathering for the 100-meter hurdle.

"If we don't get our runner to the first event in forty-five seconds," Beck said, "we'll have to forfeit!"

"No!" Karl shouted, as his shorts twisted and he fell over. The Scream Team athletes couldn't lose tonight. If they did, they'd never get invited to the Deadcathlon, and his plan to help the Conundrums would fail. Plus, Alphonse would think he was right to call them losers.

Karl's mind raced. "Patsy can do it!"

"Uh, I don't know if you noticed, Karl," Patsy said. "I'm kind of a pile of zombie over here."

"I'll have her back together in no time," Maxwell said. He shuffled over and screwed one of her hands into her leg just above the knee.

Karl wiggled over to Patsy's head. "You can do this," he told her. "You're the only one who isn't wearing a boa-worm uniform."

"I don't know," she whispered, and blushed. That was something that Karl had never seen her do. "I haven't been able to cross the finish line once, not even in practice, without exploding."

Karl smiled. "That's not a problem. You've already exploded."

Before Patsy could respond, Alphonse shouted from the track, "Come on, losers! Get over here so we can beat you!"

When Patsy hesitated, Karl said, "Everyone has a part to play on a team . . . only this time you'll have to use every part to play."

This made Patsy laugh. "Okay, Karl," she finally said. "I'll give it a shot."

# CHAPTER 3
## PLAYING THE PARTS

While the rest of her body stayed with the Scream Team, Patsy sent her leg with the hand on top out to the starting line. The Werewolves were waiting there for Frank the Cyclops, the referee, to signal the start to the 100-meter dash.

"What's this mess all about?" Alphonse said, laughing when he saw Patsy's hand and leg bouncing toward them. "This has to be against the rules!"

Frank the ref flipped through the rule book. His one giant eye scanned the pages, but he didn't see anything that said monsters couldn't compete in pieces.

"Fine," Alphonse said. "If this is how Karl and his friends want to lose today, that works for us."

Next week, the Deadcathlon would have Spins, or surprise twists, on each event. That was what made it special. But tonight's meet against the Werewolves was like others during the regular season. It just had regular races and events.

Alphonse, two other Werewolves, and Patsy's leg lined up in the starting blocks. Frank fired the starting cannon and off they went!

The hand on top made Patsy's leg sound like a spring. *Boing! Boing! Boing!* The leg bounded over the ten hurdles, easily clearing them all, and finished way ahead of the Werewolves.

"First place!" Karl yelled. "Way to go, Patsy!"

In the high jump, Patsy used her calf and wrist to spring into her approach. She took off, soared over the bar, and landed calf-first on the mat.

For the discus throw, she anchored the toes of one foot into the ground and put her arm on the foot's heel. Then she picked up the discus and spun

her arm around like a sprinkler. She released the discus at just the right second. It flew down the field and put her in first place.

Patsy's parts were like customized machines, made especially to win the events.

But then she started running out of parts. Her shoulder couldn't do much with the javelin, and her left hip wasn't too great at the shot put. The Werewolves easily took those events.

The pole vault was the last event. And the Scream Team and the Werewolves were tied. The only thing Patsy had left to use was her head.

Just as Patsy rolled her noggin out to the pole-vault runway, Mr. Benedict announced, "The fried fungi is ready!"

He smeared the Scream Team's uniforms with a goopy reddish mess. The boa worms stopped squishing the team, and instantly the clothes loosened. Karl could breathe again.

"Patsy, it's okay!" he called. "The rest of the team can help now!"

"Too late!" Alphonse yelled. "She's not allowed to stop after she starts her turn! Looks like the Scream Team will lose . . . again!"

Karl thought Alphonse might be right. Patsy was pushing her head down the pole-vault runway with her tongue. Her head rolled and smacked into one end of the pole. She grabbed on to it with her teeth. The pole slid for an inch before catching in the ground and tilting up. Her head was catapulted through the air.

As Patsy soared across the night sky, she glanced down at the Werewolves. "Sorry, Alphonse, did you say something? Looks like the Scream Team is a little a*head* of you now, doesn't it?"

Patsy easily cleared the bar. Her head bounced onto the mattress stuffed with dried pus bags—and the Scream Team won the meet!

At first, Karl and the rest of the team were too shocked to move. They were so used to losing and disappointment.

Then *blam!* They all rushed out to the field. They grabbed Patsy's laughing head and tossed it in the air. Even after they put her pieces back together, she was still laughing. "I just wish the Coaches Conundrum were around to join in the celebration!" she said.

After hurrying through the handshake line, Alphonse and the Werewolves hustled onto their bus. As he watched them drive off, Karl got excited again. "We might actually win the Deadcathlon and the Conundrum Cup," he said. "We're going to break the Conundrum Cup Curse!"

J.D. turned bright red. "Karl!"

"What?" Karl asked. "What bad thing could happen now? We won!"

"Um, I think not," a voice said, from up on the bleachers. As the monsters turned to look, a figure stepped out from between the creatures with the purple robes. Dennis shrieked and flew straight up. The rest of the Scream Team gasped.

It was none other than Dr. Neuron!

Karl wished he'd never opened his mouth. Dr. Neuron was president of the JCML, and he had spent the last few sports seasons trying to destroy the Scream Team.

Anytime something good happened to them, Dr. Neuron would show up to make it bad. And after things went bad, he would make them worse. Dr. Neuron couldn't stand that the Scream Team was made up of different types of monsters. He thought it should all be one kind, like other JCML teams.

Dr. Neuron cleared his throat. "The tragedy that occurred here tonight is not what the Junior Club

Monster League is all about," he said, as if talking to a crowd of a thousand monsters instead of just a handful. "Luckily, I'm here to fix the situation and give you a choice."

"Does *fix* mean 'ruin'?" Patsy asked.

"Does *choice* mean 'kick in the head'?" Beck asked.

"Oh, you monsters are so terribly charming," Dr. Neuron said, through clenched teeth. "Here's the first option. You can keep tonight's victory and not get invited to next week's Deadcathlon."

Karl said, "What's the second choice?"

"Or . . ." Dr. Neuron answered, sounding like the host of the game show *The Lice Is Right*. "Hitherto and henceforth, monsters must cross the finish line or complete an event as whole creatures, or their entire team will forfeit all meets forever, back and forward in time."

"I don't get it," Beck said.

"It means, I can't win the only way I can win," Patsy said. "I can't be in pieces."

"If you accept this new rule, all teams in the JCML will be invited to the world-famous Deadcathlon next week," Dr. Neuron said. "Including the Scream Team."

"Whash?" Dennis asked. The Scream Team still didn't understand his point.

Dr. Neuron sighed. "The choice is simple. Take tonight's victory and don't go to the Deadcathlon. Or accept the new rule and go to the Deadcathlon."

In a flash, Karl howled, "We choose the Deadcathlon!"

"Monstrous," Dr. Neuron said, with a wicked grin.

"No!" Patsy said. "That's not fair! That means we didn't win tonight!"

Dr. Neuron ignored her. For some reason, he nodded to the five monsters in purple robes in the bleachers. Then Dr. Neuron scurried into his waiting limo, which squealed out of the parking lot.

Karl pumped a paw in the air. This was going to be great! The winner of the Deadcathlon would receive the Conundrum Cup.

"Patsy, I know you're nervous about crossing the finish line without exploding," he said, turning toward her. But she wasn't there. "Where's Patsy?" he asked.

Bolt shrugged. "Patsy leave."

Mike said, "She ran off right after you said you'd rather be in the Deadcathlon than keep the victory today."

Karl couldn't believe it. Patsy was gone. And, of course, so were the Coaches Conundrum.

"There's only one way to set things right and fix the Scream Team," he said. "We have to win the

Conundrum Cup and destroy the Conundrum Cup Curse!"

*Ka-klam!* The stage holding the twelve-piece orchestra collapsed, creating a rattling, ringing, jangling pile of monsters and their instruments.

"Would you PLEASE stop saying that?" J.D. said.

# CHAPTER 4
## WAY TO PASS THE GAS

Three nights after the meet against the Werewolves, Karl and the whole Scream Team met up to practice in the haunted bog.

*Well, almost the whole Scream Team*, Karl thought.

The Coaches Conundrum were still fighting in their mansion, Mr. Benedict was busy searching for new uniforms, and Patsy was nowhere to be found.

None of the monsters was into the practice without Patsy. Instead of working on his sprints, Dennis played with his pet rotten tomato, Squishy. And Bolt's arm, which had belonged to a gardener, was busy plucking different mutant bog plants.

"Bolt miss Patsy," Bolt groaned.

"Me, too," Karl said. "We need her to win the Deadcathlon and break the Conundrum Cup Cu—"

J.D. flew into Karl's mouth to stop him from finishing that last word, and then popped back out.

"Blach!" Karl said, rubbing ghost off his tongue. "What's the big deal with this C-U-R-S-E?"

"Like I said, no one knows!" J.D. answered, wiping werewolf spit off his neck.

"The Conundrums must know," Karl said. "Let's convince Patsy to meet us at their mansion."

"I'll call her," Maxwell said. "Patsy and I are best friends." He started talking into a Venus elephant-trap plant, thinking it was a cell phone.

In a second, the plant had Maxwell's head in its mouth. After prying Maxwell free, Karl left Patsy a message, telling her it was an emergency and to meet them at the Conundrums'. Then Karl led the team out of the bog toward the coaches' mansion.

Halfway there, Karl spotted Patsy alone in a field

of angry grass. She hadn't seen Karl and the other monsters yet. They watched as she created a line out of snot snakes on the grass. She stepped back and she started sprinting toward the line, moving faster than the wind!

*Go, Patsy, go!* Karl thought.

Then, just an inch before the finish line . . . Patsy exploded. Her body parts burst apart like fireworks during the annual Night of Decay Celebration.

"Come on, guys," Karl said. The Scream Team scattered, each monster grabbing one of her parts. Bolt found her head in a pus-bag tree. When they all met in the middle of the field, Patsy's face looked embarrassed and angry.

"What are you doing here?" she demanded.

"You don't need to do this on your own, Patsy," Karl said as they fitted her back together. "Let's work on it as a team."

"Work on what?" Patsy asked stubbornly.

"Remember when we started the Scream Team?" he asked. "It was because we were done being

afraid. Right?"

"I'm not scared!" Patsy said, but didn't sound convincing. When they had her back in one piece, she finally said, "Okay, I'm not the kind of zombie who gives up without a fight. I got your message. You're right. I think we need the Conundrums to help us. Let's go!"

She stomped off. Karl and the other monsters hurried to catch up. When they arrived at the haunted mansion, the drawbridge was already down. They crossed over the moat of bubbling, burping pond scum.

Karl gave the towering front door a push. It

creaked open and the Scream Team stepped into the dark hallway.

"Hello?" Beck asked nervously.

As the monsters' eyes adjusted to the darkness, they could see that a thick strip of orange *duck* tape ran through the middle of everything. It cut the floor in half and then ran up the walls. Even the chandelier had tape on it.

"It looks like the Conundrums split the mansion in two," Karl said. "Virgil must have taken one side and Wyatt the other."

With his teammates following, Karl crept down a long hallway. Nozzles along one wall tracked their movement and shot bursts of gas. *Lsst! Lsst!*

"Watch out for the passing gas!" Karl warned.

Too late. Bolt took a whiff, and his ballet-dancer foot went up on tiptoes, as if trying to escape the stench. "Ugh," he groaned.

Karl nodded. "That must be Wyatt's side."

"And this must be Virgil's," Beck said, pointing to small pits and gurgling pools of acid that ran along the other side of the hallway.

The Scream Team finally made it to the living room. It looked like it had once been a torture chamber. Next to a three-story-high fireplace, a large high-backed chair was turned away from them. Karl spotted the coaches in one corner, wearing their footy pajamas. They were both scribbling all over a chalkboard and, of course, fighting.

"With this hurdling technique, we'll score for sure," Virgil said.

"No!" Wyatt cried. "This new technique will get rid of the chance that we won't score."

Karl rolled his eyes. They were making the same argument. All this fighting over track or field must be why they didn't come to practice.

"Hi, Coaches," Patsy said.

Virgil's face lit up when he saw the Scream Team. "What's up, dudes? I don't see my brother around. Feel free to rap with me about anything."

"I'm right here!" Wyatt snapped.

Virgil's half of the body jumped. "Stop sneaking

up on me!" he said with a laugh.

Karl had to get them to focus. "Coaches Conundrum, Patsy needs your help—"

"Not just me!" Patsy insisted.

Karl started again. "We need your help to win the Deadcathlon and the Conundrum Cup."

Virgil nodded. "Dude, that's why I was just going to invite you all over."

"That was my idea!" Wyatt said. "Even though you might all be spies!"

Before Karl could respond, the high-backed chair next to the fire spun around. "Hee-hoo-hee!" the monster in the chair said.

Karl was stunned. "Happy, is that you?"

"Abso-tootly!" Happy cried, with a huge grin.

# CHAPTER 5
# THE TALE OF THE CONUNDRUMS

Happy was Dr. Neuron's nephew. He had tried to destroy the Scream Team during football season . . . at least in the beginning. He looked like a smaller Dr. Neuron, and he was a crunch-bug puppeteer.

"What are you doing here, Happy?" Beck asked.

"I hired him," Virgil said.

"No, I hired him!" Wyatt said.

"Hired him for what?" Patsy interrupted.

"I have started Happy's Crunch-Bug Puppet Theater Dramatic Reenactments," Happy said, pointing to the corner. There sat a small puppet stage on a toy wagon. "I'm taking my traveling puppet show on the road tomorrow. Before I go, the coaches wanted me to show you what happened all those years ago at the first Deadcathlon."

As the other monsters took their seats, Happy dimmed the lights and plopped a flashlight into Eric so it pointed at the stage like a spotlight.

Happy stepped behind the stage and said in a deep voice, "I give you the *Tale of the Conundrums!*" Using little paddles, he pushed two crunch bugs out onto the stage. The bugs were tied together by a loose piece of thread and meandered here and there.

"We're the Conundrums!" Happy said, throwing his voice to sound like the bugs were talking.

"No, we're the Conundrums!" Wyatt yelled from the audience, and Virgil chirped, "Yes, we're us."

"This is a play," Karl explained. "Happy's acting like the crunch bugs are you two."

"That's easy to believe." Virgil laughed. "That actor looks just like you, Wyatt."

"Stop bugging me!" Wyatt snapped.

Happy continued with his show. He made his voice sound chipper like Virgil's and moved one of the bugs. "I sure am glad we've brought our team here to the very first Deadcathlon! Aren't you, my dear brother and my best friend, Wyatt?"

"You betcha!" Happy switched to using Wyatt's voice. "We're such good coaches and buddies they even named the Conundrum Cup after us! Isn't it super fun to be brothers?"

J.D. shook his head. "*You betcha? Super fun?* That's not how Coach Wyatt talks. This is all wrong!"

But Karl noticed that for once the Conundrums weren't arguing about a part of the play. Karl wondered if it was possible that, before that first

Deadcathlon, the Conundrums might have actually agreed on things.

Happy put some curdled mayonnaise on the stage as bait, and the largest crunch bug Karl had ever seen lumbered out onto the stage.

"I am Wolfenstein!" Happy said in an even deeper voice. "I run track and field for the Conundrums."

"Wolfenstein!" Karl's tail started wagging. Wolfenstein was his all-time sports hero. Karl had forgotten that the Conundrums had been his first coaches and taught him everything he knew.

"I am not yet a star," Happy said, as Wolfenstein. "But I'm all set to run and participate in every single track-and-field event if you would like, Coaches Conundrum!"

"No," the Virgil bug said. "Wolfenstein, you must share the glory, just as my brother and I share everything, including ideas and views on life."

The Wyatt bug cried, "I agree!"

The Scream Team gasped. Karl had been right! The Conundrums used to agree with each other!

Happy pressed a button on a speaker. A short burst of music played, like when a movie bad guy pops up on the screen. A new crunch bug skittered onstage.

"I'm the water boy for the Conundrums' team," Happy said in a voice that sounded familiar to Karl but he couldn't quite place. "The rest of the team wanted me to tell you that they don't want to participate. You are making a mistake if you don't let Wolfenstein run and play in every event. He will make the JCML great!"

"No, water boy," the Virgil bug said. "It's never a

mistake to include everyone on the team. Let's keep warming up!"

A group of crunch bugs dressed in track uniforms crawled onstage. Happy had tied miniprops, like fake hurdles and pole-vault bars, to his tentacles. He dangled the props and pushed the team of crunch bugs into them.

The crunch bugs crashed into the props and each other, and flipped over. Happy kept talking as the water boy. "Coaches Conundrum, the decision you made to use the other athletes has gone horribly

wrong! Now they're all injured. Pervis thought the javelin toss was a javelin-eating contest. Mervis accidentally put a sock on his head and ran into every single hurdle. And Alexis's braids got so twisted in the pole-vault poles that she looks like a porcupine. Those players will never be heard from again. And you, Coaches Conundrum, will be cursed and must never set foot on the track at the Deadcathlon again!"

Happy finally stopped here, waiting for a big reaction. But the Scream Team just looked confused.

"That water-boy character has too many lines," Maxwell said. "The whole dramatic structure is flawed."

Karl didn't know about that. The play wasn't so great, but the real Conundrums in the audience weren't helping things. They started acting even more strangely than usual.

Virgil said, "The water boy was definitely taller in real life, Happy dude!"

"All wrong, Happy!" Wyatt instructed. "There was more smog that night!"

Happy tried to change the action on the stage, and accidentally smeared curdled mayonnaise everywhere. The crunch-bug actors went berserk and started chomping on the set. It collapsed around Happy, and soon he was buried in the wreckage. At last, he announced, "The end!"

Patsy exploded.

"Come on!" she said, as her head sailed toward the acne aquarium. "Now I'm even exploding at the finish of a bad play? No offense, Happy!"

But Happy didn't seem to care. "Hee-ho-hee!" he said. The team got to work gathering up Patsy's parts from around the room.

"That's it?" J.D. said. "I still don't understand what the Conundrum Cup C-U-R-S-E is!"

Karl shook his head. "Neither do I."

"The message is totally clear," Coach Wyatt said. "I'm not going to the Deadcathlon this weekend."

"Wrong-o!" Coach Virgil said. "The Deadcathlon is not a place I'll be going to this weekend, either."

"But you have to!" Karl said, thinking about

Alphonse, Dr. Neuron, and everyone else who didn't believe in the team. "We need to win the Conundrum Cup to prove we're not losers!"

"Too many monsters could get hurt," Virgil said, and looked at Patsy. "That's why I can't tell you to run if you don't want to."

"No," Wyatt snapped. "That's why if you want to not run I can't tell you to, Patsy."

Once again, the Conundrums didn't realize they were saying the same thing. But Patsy seemed to hear them loud and clear.

"They're right, Karl," Patsy said. "I'm not going, either. I wanted the coaches to teach me a lesson, and they did. I shouldn't even try to cross the finish line anymore. It's not worth it!" Patsy ran out of the room.

"Wow, she's fast," Mike said.

It was true, Karl thought, looking around at the mess. Patsy could help them win the Deadcathlon.

But with her gone and the Conundrums refusing to coach, was the show over for the Scream Team?

# CHAPTER 6
## THE AWFUL OVAL

"Welcome, fiends and ghouls, to the annual JCML Deadcathlon!"

The shout made Karl jump. He'd been giving the Scream Team a pre-meet pep talk near the pole vault and turned around to find the meet announcer, Hairy Hairwell. Usually, Hairy would be in a skybox above the stands. But this year he was walking around the track, with an assistant lugging his sound equipment behind him. Karl figured Hairy must have wanted to get a closer look at the events.

"I'm coming to you live from the Awful Oval on the floor of Putridge Stadium!" Hairy's voice echoed around the stadium. "We're just five minutes from the start of the biggest, most spectacular sporting event of the year! It's a two-day meet, with all the teams of the JCML competing in four events one day and five the second day . . . ending, of course, with the big Monster Relay Race!"

Cheers burst from the thousands of monsters who packed the stands. Even with the Conundrums and Patsy not showing up, Karl felt a jolt of happy excitement. Ever since he was a tiny cub, Karl had loved the Deadcathlon.

There was always something new and nutty happening. The point of the Deadcathlon was that each event had a special twist. And that twist was decided by the mysterious purple-robed creatures who were called Spinners.

In fact, the night before, the Spinners had set up purple curtains all around the stadium near the different events. At the beginning of each event, the curtain would be pulled back to reveal the surprise.

One year, the wrong jump became the *very, very* wrong jump, in which athletes leapt over graves. The pole vault was the slime-pail vault. And instead of hurdling, there was a contest to see who could make the loudest blood-curdling screams.

"I'm looking for a team that might be able to make a showing of things today," Hairy Hairwell said, looking right at the Scream Team. "But I just don't see one."

Trying to get his attention, Eric bounced up and down and Mike waved his tail like a flag.

"Nope, still don't see a team worth talking to," Hairy said. "Oh! There!"

He pushed past the Scream Team and walked over to Alphonse and the other Werewolves, who were warming up near their high-tech bus. As the winners of the trophy last year, the Werewolves still held on to the Conundrum Cup.

"There it is!" Karl said, peering through the Werewolves' bus's window. The cup was made of

rusted metal. He moved through the crowd so he could get a closer look. The handles on the sides were shaped like the Conundrums' faces: One looked like Virgil and the other, Wyatt.

"Alphonse, Dr. Neuron has called you the next Wolfenstein," Hairy said. "What's your goal in this year's Deadcathlon?"

Alphonse didn't seem to realize there wasn't a camera and kept flexing his arm muscles as he answered. "My goal is to push my inner monster, body and brain, to the last drop of energy."

*Oh brother*, Karl thought, but Hairy seemed to be eating it up.

"That's the answer of a true winner," Hairy said. "Since the tragic events of the first Deadcathlon, the Werewolves have taken home the Conundrum Cup more than any other team. I have no doubt that their winning record will continue!"

Alphonse and the rest of the Werewolves howled just as the five Spinners shuffled out to the center of the field.

"What are they doing?" Beck asked.

"It's part of a Deadcathlon tradition," J.D. said. "At the start, all teams have to sign up for the last event, the Monster Relay."

The Scream Team went over one by one to sign up. Karl waited until he thought no one was looking and then added another name under his own. Beck spotted what he was doing and pointed to the extra name.

"You put Patsy's name on the relay list, Karl?" Beck asked. "But she's not coming, right?"

J.D.'s eyes bugged out in shock. "The Monster Relay is worth five times the points of any other

event!" he said. "When she doesn't show up, we'll lose the Deadcathlon for sure."

Karl didn't want to hear it. "We have to get Patsy back so we can win the Conundrum Cup as a team," he said stubbornly. "Then the coaches will stop fighting and we'll finally break the—"

"Don't say it!" J.D. warned.

But Karl was too worked up to stop. He shouted, "Conundrum Cup Curse!"

*Kaboom!* A cannon fired. J.D. ducked. But it was just the starting cannon, and the crowd in the stands cheered. The Deadcathlon was officially underway!

# CHAPTER 7
## SPINNING OUT OF CONTROL

"The spooky-yard dash will be the first Deadcathlon event!" Hairy announced.

Dennis would run the race for the Scream Team, and Karl thought for sure he'd come in at least second place. Dennis might not beat the runner from the Sea Monsters. But if he could just keep a straight line from the starting block to the finish line once his tiny wings started flapping, he'd be all set.

"As the racers line up on the starting blocks, the Spinners are coming out to the track to reveal the Spin on this event," Hairy said.

The five purple-robed creatures pulled a cord. The curtain that ran along the track lifted, showing the surprise they had planned for the spooky-yard dash. Raw red meat sat in each lane of the track.

"The Spinners have replaced the starting blocks with steaks!" Hairy announced.

"Osh nosh!" Dennis blurted, freaking out. "Did he say *stakes*?"

Just then the cannon fired, starting the race. Dennis shot straight up. If the finish line had been in the sky, he would have won. As it was, Mabel of the Sea Monsters easily took first place, and James of the Frankenstein's Monsters came in second, with Kevin of the Werewolves taking third.

"Shorry!" Dennis slurred, after he crash-landed next to the Scream Team.

"That's okay," Karl told him. "It's just bad luck that the Spinners picked the one thing you're most scared of. We'll do better in the next event, the high jump."

"The high jump is my event," J.D. said

confidently. "I've totally got this one!"

The teams moved down the stadium floor to the high-jump area. This time, the Spinners' purple curtain was right in front of the mat. It covered the two poles that held the high-jump bar.

"There are unpredictable gusting winds tonight!" Hairy shouted. "So all the teams are really going to have to time the approach just right."

"No problem," J.D. said, giving Karl a high five. "I'll float right over the bar."

The five Spinners moved in. The curtain was lifted. Instead of the bar across the two upright poles, a thin rope stretched across the space.

"Is that a clothesline?" J.D. asked, making gagging sounds and turning green. "I feel kind of . . ."

"Yeah, I can see that." Karl watched the food in J.D.'s stomach begin to swirl and then head north. It was clear he'd eaten a banana and cereal for breakfast.

"Looks like someone ate his Wheezies," Alphonse said with a laugh.

Ever since the Vampires had hypnotized J.D. during basketball season and turned him into a sheet, he'd been terrified of anything to do with laundry. Fabric softener, dryer lint, and . . . clotheslines.

"I don't know if I can do it," J.D. said, "but I'll give it a try." As he got closer to the takeoff point, his body went flat and draped over the clothesline. He flapped there for a while as the crowd laughed and jeered.

Alphonse snickered. "Looks like you can put the Scream Team to bed!"

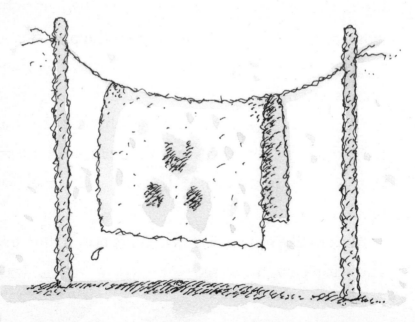

Finally, Karl trotted out and tugged on J.D. He was slightly tangled by now and Karl had to yank pretty hard. They both flew backward in a heap of fur and ghost.

As Karl brushed himself off, he thought about the Spins so far in the Deadcathlon. The steaks. The clothesline. Was it really just bad luck that the twists seemed especially focused on things that scared the Scream Team?

*It must be a coincidence*, Karl thought.

Then Karl's first event, the wrong jump, came up. He got that feeling of nibbling moths in his stomach. His legs felt rubbery from the pressure.

"What is it?" J.D. asked him, noticing Karl glancing over his shoulder.

"Something is following me!" Karl said, and he started chasing it. It was only when he heard Alphonse laughing that he realized he was chasing his own tail.

"Get it together, Karl," he told himself, and got ready for the most important jump of his life. Karl had his foolproof paw pattern. Left paw, right paw, right, right, right, left. If he could simply remember that, he'd be fine.

"Bryce of the Blobs has dominated the wrong jump for the past three Deadcathlons," Hairy announced. "Of course, Alphonse of the Werewolves is the absolute favorite and a real crowd-pleaser. But starting us off is . . . Larry of the Scream Team!"

"Nosh!" Dennis shouted. "His namesh Sharl!"

"Oh," Hairy said, and halfheartedly tried again. "Sharl of the Scream Team!"

Just as Karl took his place at the head of the wrong-jump runway, the Spinners shuffled over and pulled back the curtain. Instead of sand filling the pit, there were thousands of squeaky toys: chomping koala creatures and gnasher puppies with huge bug eyes.

*Uggie! Phlick!* The toys peeped.

Karl tried leaping over the pit, but the squeaking was too much. He tripped and fell snout-first into the heap of toys. He gave up fighting the urge, and started gnawing on a plastic three-headed sloth.

Finally, Frank the referee had to waddle over and pluck Karl out of the pit.

"Way to go, poodle," Alphonse said to Karl, before easily jumping over the pile of toys. In fact, every other monster sailed over the pit.

Karl turned to his friends. "Something's fishy. Why are the Spinners picking the exact fears of the Scream Team?"

Nobody had time to figure it out. The last event of the day was about to start, and Mike the swamp thing had to get ready.

"Next up, the pole vault!" Hairy announced.

The Spinner lifted the curtain, and revealed the

poles that would be used in the vault.

They looked just like fishing poles.

"Ahhhh!" Mike screamed. "That's the same type of rod that hooked my uncle Cedric!"

He collapsed into a sobbing heap of scales and slime. The Scream Team helped him over to the bench as the other teams vaulted.

Karl couldn't believe it. So far, the Spin in each of the events had been based solely on the weaknesses of the Scream Team. He remembered the first track meet, when Dr. Neuron had been hanging out with the purple-robed Spinners in the stands. He must have been convincing them to destroy the Scream Team!

"But why would they listen to him?" Karl asked out loud, but before he could come up with answer, Frank the Cyclops pressed a few buttons on a control pad and the stadium scoreboard read:

Zombies 8

Frankenstein's Monsters 18

Werewolves 32

Sea Monsters 10

"What's our score?" Beck asked.

"We're being trounced," J.D. said. "Our score is so low, we don't even get mentioned on the board. We have zero."

Zero. Zero. Zero.

The word echoed in Karl's mind. That was their score, and their chances of winning the Conundrum Cup and ending the curse.

# CHAPTER 8
## TWO DAY'S THE DAY

Karl woke up that night from a daymare in which he was being chased by a pack of slobbering, squeaking toys. He jumped out of bed, grabbed a bowlful of roadkill parts, and headed outside to his lair. That was what he called his tree fort in the backyard, which was where he did his best thinking.

And Karl had a lot think about. He needed to come up with a plan to get the coaches and Patsy to the second night of the Deadcathlon, which started in twenty minutes. As he snacked on the roadkill, he looked around his lair at the posters of his hero, Wolfenstein.

Why were the Spinners trying to destroy the Scream Team?

If Karl could just figure that out . . . and the twenty-year-old mystery that had driven the Conundrums into early retirement and ruined their lives and their old team, he could convince them to set foot on the track at the Deadcathlon and they could deal with the Spinners.

Then the coaches would tell Patsy to come back to the Scream Team and all would be okay again.

Karl thought about Happy's play. He knew something bad had happened to the Conundrums' first team at the first Deadcathlon, that their water boy had had a lot to say, and that Wolfenstein had become a hero because of what happened. . . .

Karl didn't have time to put all the pieces together now. He hopped on his bike and headed to the stadium.

The stands were as crowded the second and final night of the Deadcathlon. With his cell-phone camera ready to shoot, Karl trotted over to the five

hooded Spinners gathered next to the track.

"Here," he said, holding out a hunk of meat. "I saved you some roadkill."

The tallest Spinner turned to him and reached out a hand. Karl could see what looked like a javelin poking out from under the monster's hood.

"Say *roadkill*!" Karl said. *Click!* He took a quick picture of himself and the Spinner, and e-mailed it to the Conundrums. He wanted them to think everyone was now great friends at the Deadcathlon. Then maybe they'd show up.

But instead of taking the food, the Spinner snapped its fingers at Frank the referee. The ref rushed over and hustled Karl over to the waiting Scream Team.

"What was that all about?" J.D. asked.

"I thought maybe they're just hungry," Karl answered. "I can get pretty cranky when my stomach's empty."

"Are you going to eat that?" Dennis asked, eyeing the roadkill. Before Karl could answer, Dennis ate the whole thing.

"We have a real nail-biter for today's first event," Hairy Hairwell shouted over the loudspeakers. "It's the 100-meter hurdle!"

Karl and the rest of the Scream Team clapped and hooted as Bolt went to the starting line.

"Go get 'em, Bolt!" Karl said. He had a feeling that with a name like Bolt, the Frankenstein's monster would be a really fast sprinter.

When all the runners were in place, the starting cannon fired again and the Spinners pulled back the curtain they had set up next to the track. Behind it was a four-piece jazz band on a small stage. Each time a monster approached a hurdle, the band would start playing.

"Oh, that's kind of nice!" Dennis said, clapping his mini wings in time with the music.

But Karl knew it was a problem. Whenever the band played, Bolt stopped. His ballet-dancer foot would go up on pointe and he would do a little twirl.

"This is a historic night, fiends and ghouls,"

Hairy yelled as the race finally ended. "We have a new world record for Caroline of the Zombies . . . and Bolt of the Scream Team has run the slowest 100-meter hurdle in the history of monsterkind!"

"Bolt sad," Bolt said as he slunk over to weed a patch of the field. The only good news was that the Werewolves' runner, Christine, came in fifth. So their overall lead wasn't as huge.

"The javelin toss is next!" Hairy announced. "The Scream Team will go first!"

Maxwell stumbled over to an asparagus creature and tried to pick it up. "This javelin is awfully frisky!" he said. Karl guided him to the right spot and put a real javelin in his hand.

The spectators watched eagerly as the Spinners shuffled out to the curtain at the opposite end of the javelin area. With a tug, they pulled away the curtain. At first there was stunned silence as everyone looked at the Spin.

It was a jacket and a pair of pants on a hanger.

Karl didn't see the problem until he heard a spectator say, "Those colors really clash, don't they?"

Just as Maxwell turned, Karl rushed over and slid his wrapping farther down over his eyes. "Trust me, Maxwell, don't look!" Karl warned.

Maxwell couldn't resist. He moved his wrapping and his eyes locked on the pants and the jacket. "Ahh!" Maxwell shouted. "That color combination is hideous! I need to go lie down!"

The mummy stumbled over to the Scream Team bench and collapsed.

The hammer-toe event was next. This time, the Spin required that all monsters use their own toes. Eric the blob, of course, was lacking in that department. He fouled out on his first try.

When the Werewolves' Ryan came in third in the event, Hairy Hairwell announced, "This puts us in an exciting situation! The Monster Relay is worth fifty points. The winner of the relay will actually walk away the winner of the entire Deadcathlon, despite the Conundrum Cup Curse!"

J.D. cringed, waiting for something bad to happen. And this time, Karl cringed, too.

"Hey there, Scream Team buddies!" Virgil Conundrum said.

Dennis shrieked and shot up into the air, where he ricocheted around the stadium lights like a pinball. Karl turned to see the Conundrums behind them. They were standing on stilts. Karl figured it was because they were scared to actually set foot on the track at the Deadcathlon.

"You're here!" Karl said happily.

Wyatt nodded. "Just don't tell Virgil I'm here if you see him. He's been following me everywhere!"

"Where's the zombie in that photo you sent, Karl?" Virgil asked. "I have to talk to him!"

"Why?" Karl asked. There wasn't much time before the start of the relay race.

Wyatt started to say, "That picture is why I'm here at—" when Dennis fell out of the sky and struck the Conundrums, toppling them off their stilts and onto the track.

Screams of panic erupted around the stadium.

"The Conundrums have set foot onto the track at the Deadcathlon!" Hairy screeched over the speakers. "Run for your lives or your undeaths!"

The coaches tried to balance up on their toes as if that would be better than their full feet on the track. For a split second, they teetered, and then fell over sideways, landing directly on top of the Spinner who had snapped his fingers at Frank in front of Karl.

*Umph!* They all hit the ground together.

The silence was filled by a coughing sound. A piece of rotten wood freed itself from inside the Spinner's purple robes. It rolled away down the track and rattled to a halt in front of the stands.

"What is that?" a spiderbot in the bleachers asked.

A nearby sea monster shouted, "It's a piece of javelin from about twenty years ago!"

Virgil's eyes went wide as he gazed down at the Spinner.

Wyatt demanded, "Is that you, Pervis?"

# CHAPTER 9
## RULES OF THE SHAME

"No, no," the robed monster said weakly, clearly lying. "I'm not Pervis. I'm just a mysterious Spinner! I certainly don't know you from the past or hold any kind of grudge against you!"

Dr. Neuron started rushing down from his skybox. Karl had never seen him move so fast. "Leave that Spinner, who has no name, alone!" he demanded, as he hurried their way.

The Conundrums ignored him and pulled back the monster's purple hood, revealing a zombie underneath. He had three pieces of javelin stuck in his mouth, like oversize teeth.

"It *is* you, Pervis!" Virgil said, astounded, as the Conundrums and the zombie climbed to their feet.

Karl couldn't believe his eyes. Could this be the same Pervis from Happy's play about the Deadcathlon?

"Yes, it's me," the zombie said angrily. Pervis tried covering up his face again. But Wyatt stopped him and asked, "What about the rest of the Spinners? Do we know them, too?"

Before the four other robed creatures could stop them, Wyatt and Virgil pulled back their hoods. Karl could see a bigfoot with pole vaults stuck in her braid so she looked like a porcupine, a ghost with a tube sock pulled over his head, a sea monster, and a Frankenstein's monster.

For the first time, Karl heard Wyatt gasp. "It's Alexis and Mervis," he said. "And the other players from our team twenty years ago, at the first Deadcathlon!"

"Ahhhh, cover up their faces again!" Dr. Neuron shouted when he reached the track. "They're hideous!"

"They look great to me!" Maxwell said. "The purple robes really bring out their twenty-year-old track injuries."

Dr. Neuron scoffed. "There is nothing more hideous than failure."

"He's right!" Mervis said. "We are grotesque. And it's all thanks to the Conundrums!"

Dennis flitted over and gently pulled one of the javelin parts from Pervis's mouth. He popped it into his own. "Mmmm," he said. "Perfectly aged."

"Bolt sick." Bolt turned green and keeled over.

Karl yanked a piece of the pole vault out of Alexis's braid. "This stuff comes right out. Didn't you ever bother trying to fix yourselves up?"

"Why does it matter?" Pervis said. "We aren't worth the effort. For twenty years, Dr. Neuron has told us we should wear these purple robes to hide our shame. He said that the Conundrums didn't want us to run in the first Deadcathlon and planned our injuries during the warm-up. And that they spent every second of every day laughing about it!"

Dr. Neuron turned his head and giggled. When the Conundrums and the Scream Team glared at him, he acted like he was coughing.

"It's totally the opposite," Karl said. "The Conundrums have spent every second since that day fighting, not laughing. Just look at them!"

For the first time, Pervis seemed to really check out the Conundrums. He stared at Wyatt's cranky expression and Virgil's goofy "whatever" look.

"Have we been wrong all these years?" Pervis asked. "Dr. Neuron said the best way for us to get revenge was to Spin each event in the Deadcathlon against the Scream Team. That way, you'd lose every event so awfully that you'd never want to compete again."

"Like us," Mervis said. "We're horrible."

"And they are horrible, aren't they?" Dr. Neuron turned to the crowd. "Don't you think so? They were a team of different monsters. I hated it then, I hate it now. We need a winner like Alphonse to make the JCML great! He'll be the next Wolfenstein!"

The words *make the JCML great* hit Karl like a lightning bolt. He had heard the same words in Happy's play.

"I should have known it!" Karl shouted. "Dr. Neuron was the water boy! That's why his voice sounded so familiar in the play!"

"So what?" Dr. Neuron didn't try to deny it. "Everyone has to start somewhere."

Karl was putting it all together. "You wanted the Conundrums' team to fail, because that way Wolfenstein would win and create a huge name for the JCML! You used his success to turn yourself from water boy into the president of the league!"

"Wow, Karl." J.D. whistled. "That's impressive."

"But now that we know the truth, it's

too late," Pervis said. "And we saved the worst Spin for the Monster Relay Race."

"What is the Spin?" Karl asked.

Pervis shook his head. "I can't tell you that or change the Spin now," he said. "It's against the rules. But I can tell you that we chose just the right Spin to make sure that the Scream Team will lose the relay race today and will never want to be a team again."

Dr. Neuron smiled. "And the Conundrum Cup C-U-R-S-E will continue forever!"

"There is no Conundrum Cup Curse!" Karl yelled.

As he said the last three words, the crowd gasped. J.D. turned red. Dennis shrieked. But . . . nothing bad happened.

"See?" Karl said. "The curse doesn't exist!"

Dr. Neuron shrugged. "All that matters is that after today's Deadcathlon, the Scream Team will be so filled with shame they'll be just like these Spinners," he said. "Now come with me, Pervis. We have to start the Monster Relay Race in exactly one minute. I want to get ready to crown Alphonse and the rest of the Werewolves as the official winners."

After Dr. Neuron stomped off, taking the confused-looking Spinners with him, Karl turned to the Scream Team.

"Patsy needs to know there is no curse," he said. "I have to go find her."

"But the race is about to start!" J.D. said. His body turned even more red with alarm. "There's no time!"

"The race has nine laps," Karl said. "I'm supposed to run the eighth lap. That gives me a couple of minutes."

Still, J.D. shook his head. "Karl, you'll never make it. Her house is too far away."

"I owe her for choosing the Deadcathlon over her win," Karl said. "I have to try! And we need to run this race together, otherwise we'll never be a real team."

Virgil's half of the body stepped toward him. "Don't worry, dude," he said. "I'll drive you to Patsy in my van."

"No," Wyatt said. "I'll drive you in my van!"

Time ticked by as the brothers fought. The runners from the other teams were heading to the starting line.

Finally, J.D. shook his head and threw his hands in the air. "Just go on your bike, Karl! Go find Patsy and bring her back. Hurry!"

# CHAPTER 10
## MONSTER RELAY

Karl darted over to his bike and hopped on. As he pedaled away from the stadium, he clicked on the radio strapped to bike's handlebars. Hairy Hairwell was already announcing from the starting line.

"Welcome to the Monster Relay here at the Putridge Stadium Awful Oval! This final event of the Deadcathlon has nine laps. Each team will race nine monsters, one monster per lap. It's a chance for the Scream Team to actually do something, after failing so, so, so miserably in earlier events."

*Thanks a lot*, Karl thought. He turned down

Mange Street and nearly crashed into an oozing hydrant.

On the radio, Hairy Hairwell was getting even more excited. "The Scream Team is up against one of the best lineups I can remember seeing. The Sea Monsters and the Frankenstein's Monsters are very fast. Looking as confident and dashing as ever, Alphonse of the Werewolves is getting down onto his starting blocks with the other runners!"

Karl didn't need the radio to hear the starting cannon. It echoed out of the stadium and bounced off the stores on either side of the street.

"And away they go!" Hairy yelled. "The Werewolves' Alphonse has a clear lead as they come around the first bend. Beck the bigfoot of the Scream Team is using what can only be described as a spatula technique, as he flippers along the track."

"Don't trip, Beck, don't trip!" Karl said out loud, just as Hairy shouted, "And Beck the bigfoot has tripped! It's a heap of rolling feet. Oh, the monstrosity!"

Karl listened as Beck got back to his feet, finished his lap, and handed off the baton to J.D.

"The racers are fairly even except for J.D. of the Scream Team, who's way in the back," Hairy said over the radio. "Thanks to Alphonse, the Werewolves are well positioned as they head into the second leg! But the Sea Monsters are giving them a run for their money!"

*Come on, J.D. You can do it!* Karl thought, spotting the sign for the Moldy Thumb up ahead.

"J.D. of the Scream Team is actually gaining some ground!" Hairy bellowed so loud that Karl nearly skidded off the road. "J.D. is making the handoff to Dennis the vampire, as the Scream Team starts the third leg of the race!"

Karl swerved into Patsy's driveway as the Werewolves increased their lead. The Sea Monsters were in second, Blobs in third, and way in the back was the Scream Team.

"Even more *way* back," Hairy announced, "because Dennis the vampire has stopped to gnaw on a wooden hurdle."

"What?" Karl could hear Dennis ask, with his mouth full of hurdle. "Imsh shtarving!"

Karl jumped off his bike and rushed to her front door. The runners would be starting the fourth leg of the relay soon. Karl had to hurry up and get back in time to run his lap.

"Patsy!" Karl shouted as he rang the doorbell. No answer. He sprinted to the backyard. She wasn't there, either.

*Wolfsbane!* Karl was running out of time.

Finally, he checked the garage. There she was!

Patsy was leaning over the wheel of her broken bicycle, trying to fix two spokes using parts of her arm.

"Karl!" Patsy said. "Am I glad to see you! I was trying to get to the race. But my bike is busted!"

"What changed your mind?" Karl asked.

"I thought about Happy's play," Patsy said. "And how all the athletes on the Conundrums' first team were different, like us. They let other monsters tear them apart."

"But we're different," Karl said.

"You got it," Patsy agreed. "We're a team, no matter what, like the Conundrums. Even if we don't agree, we need to stick together."

Karl nodded. He knew there wasn't time. But he had to say something. "I'm sorry I picked the Deadcathlon over your win," he said.

"Thanks," she said. "But now I'm kind of glad you did. I don't know if I can run across the finish or not, but I'm not going to give up without a fight!"

Karl grinned. "Let's go!"

They sprinted out to Karl's bike in the driveway. Patsy sat behind Karl on the seat and he started pedaling faster than he ever had. On the radio, they listened to Hairy.

Dennis must have handed off the baton to Mike, and Mike to Bolt at some point, because Hairy was just announcing, "There's no way the Scream Team is going to win this event, as Bolt hands off the baton to Eric the blob for the sixth lap!"

"You know what that means, Karl?" Patsy asked. "Eric is about to hand off to Maxwell. And he's supposed to hand off to . . ."

Karl got it. "He supposed to hand off to me, and I'm not there!"

Patsy unscrewed one of her legs. She used it like a gondola pole to help push them along as Karl pedaled. They zipped into the stadium parking lot and under the bleachers. Even before they'd screeched to a complete halt, the two jumped off the bike and sprinted toward the track.

"There's Patsy and Karl!" J.D. shouted. He was standing with the rest of the Scream Team near the wrong jump. The team cheered, and Patsy gave a funny bow, but Karl didn't even have time to wave.

With his wrapping over his eyes, Maxwell stumbled around the last bend of his lap. He was heading diagonally up the straightaway. Without wasting another second, Karl yelled, "Here I am, Maxwell!" and got in place to take the handoff.

When he was about twenty yards away, Maxwell tripped and the baton flew out of his hand. It made a squeaking sound as it left Maxwell's fingers.

"The Scream Team's baton is going into the stands!" Hairy shouted. For once, Karl let himself enjoy the sound. He leapt through the air. His teeth came down on the baton with a satisfying *clang*.

Karl landed on the track, and instantly his paws started pumping, moving his body forward.

"Run, Karl, run!" J.D. shouted.

As Karl began the eighth leg, he realized the Spinners still hadn't revealed the Spin. It must be something in the ninth leg. He just hoped the Scream Team would even make it to the final lap.

Right now he was half a lap behind all the other runners, who were bunched up together.

To make things worse, Alphonse started trotting along the field next to Karl. He had already run his leg of the race but he couldn't resist teasing Karl.

"Looks like it's all over for you, poodle," he sneered, with the same old smirk on his face. "You don't have what it takes to be a winner!"

"Maybe not," Karl huffed as he ran. "But I wouldn't want to win like you do, anyway!"

"Ouch." Alphonse pretended Karl had stung him. "As always, you've come in dead last."

"I think you mean he's saved the undead for last," a voice said, from the handoff point up ahead. Karl howled with happiness. It was Patsy!

Alphonse seemed so surprised to see her, he

actually tripped and fell. "Totally meant to do that!" he said.

Patsy held her arm out behind her back. Karl slapped the baton right to her. The handoff was perfect! Exhausted, Karl jogged over to the rest of his team and watched Patsy tearing down the track.

With the last handoff of the baton, it was time to reveal the Spin of the relay race.

Still in his purple robes, Pervis stepped out on the track. He gave the Scream Team a guilty look, as if he was sorry for what he was about to do. Then he lifted the curtain off the small box for the last Spin of the Deadcathlon.

Inside was a can of spray paint.

Pervis picked up the can and pointed it down. Then he made a long, white line across the track.

*Oh no*, Karl thought. *It's a finish line!*

# CHAPTER 11
# THE BIG SPIN

Karl knew it was the most horrible Spin yet.

Dr. Neuron even let out a happy little giggle. A spiderbot in the bleachers clapped all eight of its legs in excitement. An octocow mooed that it was "Utterly thrilling!" And the vendor selling hot cats dropped his tray so he could watch every horrible moment of what would happen next.

In fact, everyone in the stands leaned forward as if about to enjoy the most monstrous of meals.

They couldn't wait to see Patsy explode.

Just like everyone else in the stadium, Karl

realized that the Spinners didn't have to add any clever tricks to this Spin to make sure the Scream Team lost. The finish line itself was Patsy's biggest weakness.

"It's the ninth and final leg of the relay, and the Scream Team anchor has an impossible job to do," Hairy announced. "Not only is she half a lap behind the Sea Monster and Werewolf leaders, but she'll never get across the line."

Patsy's stride skipped a little when she saw the line.

Coach Virgil yelled, "Patsy, the line might be finished . . ."

". . . but you're not!" Coach Wyatt added.

Their words made Patsy smile. She nodded, and

her feet got back into a rhythm that was faster with each step.

Suddenly, Hairy changed his tune as he continued announcing. "Patsy of the Scream Team is making up some lost ground. She's putting on the kick!"

Karl watched Patsy blow by the Bigfoot runner, and then the Frankenstein's Monster, and she seemed to be gaining on the Sea Monster and the Werewolf.

"The zombie from the Scream Team is really giving the leaders reason to worry!" Hairy bellowed.

Maxwell shouted at the top of his lungs. "GOOOO, PATSY!"

Karl had found something he liked better than running himself: seeing his friend Patsy having so much fun again.

"The Werewolf hears Patsy catching up and he does not want to finish second in this race," Hairy yelled. "Patsy is driving through the final curve, running the turn hard. The winner is crossing the finish line!"

Karl's heart stopped as he listened for the results.

"It's Eleanor of the Sea Monsters in first!" Hairy announced. "Jeremy of the Werewolves in second, Raymond of the Blobs in third. And right behind Raymond is Patsy of the Scream Team! She's just a few yards from the finish. But will she be able to cross the line?"

"No!" a voice cried from the stands. And Karl knew it was Dr. Neuron.

"You can do it, Patsy!" Karl shouted.

She was a blur of speed, but his sharp eyes could see her foot lift to try to cross the finish line.

"Ahhhhhhhhhh!" Patsy shouted like she was about to jump into a grave full of mini mouth biters.

# CHAPTER 12
## MONSTER FINISH

Patsy's foot came down—

"Duck!" Alphonse yelled. "She's going to blow!" And a few of the Werewolves laughed and put their arms over their heads.

But when Patsy's foot touched the track and she actually crossed the finish line, the explosion was completely different from what they expected.

The cheers exploded out of the members of the Scream Team, sweeping across the field and down the track toward Patsy. She punched her fist in the air, and it stayed attached to her body.

She was in one piece!

"You did it, Patsy!" Karl let out a howl for his friend. As the Scream Team rushed to her, he glanced up at the crowd. They were already getting ready for the award ceremony and weren't cheering.

"Fourth place," Alphonse said. "Big deal."

"It *is* a big deal," Maxwell said, and wrapped Patsy in a mummy hug.

"I just thought about how the Scream Team stays together, no matter what," she said. "And I decided I could get my body to do the same!"

"Only losers would be so excited about losing," Alphonse joked.

Meanwhile, the Scream Team dumped a cooler full of boiling slime over the Conundrums. Dr. Neuron walked out to the podium.

"That was quite a race!" he said. "But the Sea Monsters are on top of the podium here, with their gold medals, and they are the winners of the Conundrum Cup. The silver goes to the Werewolves, and the bronze to Frankenstein's Monsters."

Dr. Neuron placed all the medals around the necks of the other teams, even the Werewolves, who cringed when the silver touched their fur. Using his tentacles, he extinguished the flame. "I call this year's JCML Deadcathlon to an end."

Dr. Neuron started to hurry off the stage, but Pervis held up his hand to stop him. "Wait!" he called. "You didn't award the winners of the Monster Relay Race!"

"Oh," Dr. Neuron said slyly. "I think we should talk about something else. Did you hear what the Conundrums just said about you, Pervis?"

"What did they say?" Pervis went into a daze.

Karl said. "No!"

"He's right," Pervis said, shaking himself back to reality. "No more tricks, Dr. Neuron. We're done being fooled by you. Be careful before someone drops a Spin on you."

"Fine," Dr. Neuron finally said. He went back up to the podium and tossed out a few medals to the Sea Monsters and the Werewolves.

"And that zombie from the Scream Team has . . . oh, this is ridiculous," he said, and walked away from the microphone. Something clanged to the ground as he hurried off to his waiting limo.

"It's the lead medal!" Karl trotted onto the stage and picked it up. He handed it to Pervis, who placed the medal around Patsy's neck.

The Scream Team members hooted and cheered, but they were alone. The Werewolves and the other teams were already packing up their gear and leaving the stadium.

As the medal slid on, Patsy's head popped off. The few monsters left in the crowd laughed, but Patsy didn't care.

She laughed along with them. "I didn't say I wouldn't fall to pieces every now and then, especially when I'm really happy, like right now!" she said.

The monsters on the team were a laughing, howling, cheering mob of blob, fur, fangs, wings, claws, and wrapping. Karl was glad for Patsy.

But it was hard to see the Sea Monsters carrying the Conundrum Cup away. The smallest one of them did a little dive into it and then leapt into the squirting slime in the air.

*There goes the chance I had to make the Conundrums get along again*, Karl thought glumly.

"What's the problem, Karl?" Virgil Conundrum asked. Karl turned around and saw that Wyatt and Virgil were standing right behind him.

Karl shrugged. "I thought winning that finally

would have made you two happy."

"Thanks, dude," Virgil said.

"It would have been great to win the Conundrum Cup," Wyatt said, not able to help looking cranky. "But a cup or trophy or any kind of thing isn't going to change who we are."

"We'd still be the same, with or without it," Virgil said. "Only we can decide to make a change. And I like who we are!"

Karl agreed. "I like who we are, too!"

As if the moment were too happy for him, Wyatt held out the empty cup of slime he'd been drinking from. "Here's a Conundrum Cup for you, Karl."

"Monstrous!" Karl said, laughing. He tugged the Conundrums over to the Scream Team pile and they dove in!

# Scream Team

PATSY THE ZOMBIE

**Number:** 6   Rather be 7... because 7 8 9! Ha!

**Favorite Song:** "I Fall to Pieces" by Patsy Cline
   Actually, it's "Back together Again"!

**Top Event:** Exploding
   Off of the starting block, that is!

**Best Friend:** Maxwell the mummy
   He's great to "wrap" with

**Favorite Recipe:** Patsy's finger sandwiches
   No, not MY fingers!

**Place to Improve:** Listening
   Hard when both ears fall off into a slime pit

**Favorite Finnish Line:** Pidän Aardvarks
   You mean "finish" line. I like all of them now!

**Track Hero:** Coaches Conundrum
   Better at keeping their heads than me

**Favorite Saying:** "I can do anything!"
   It's true, I can!

**Hobby:** Fixing dead engines
   I know about making things undead!